Other books by Karen Katz

Mommy Hugs

Ten Tiny Tickles

Daddy Hugs 1 2 3

Counting Christmas

Counting Kisses

Twelve Hats for Lena

Margaret K. McElderry Books

Margaret K. McElderry Books

An imprint of Simon & Schuster Children's Publishing Division

1230 Avenue of the Americas, New York, New York 10020

Copyright © 2008 by Karen Katz

Book design by Ann Bobco

The text for this book is set in Bookman Oldstyle.

The illustrations for this book are rendered in gouache, colored pencil, and collage.

Manufactured in Mexico

10 9 8 7 6 5 4

Library of Congress Cataloging-in-Publication Data

Katz, Karen.

Ten tiny babies / Karen Katz.—1st ed.

p. cm.

Summary: Babies from one to ten enjoy a bouncy, noisy, jiggly day until they are finally fast asleep at night.

ISBN-13: 978-1-4169-3546-9 (hardcover)

ISBN-10: 1-4169-3546-0 (hardcover)

[1. Babies—Fiction. 2. Counting. 3. Stories in rhyme.] I. Title.

PZ8.3.K1283Te 2008

[E]—dc22

2007036061

ten tiny babies

by karen katz

Margaret K. McElderry Books
New York • London • Toronto • Sydney

To
Ann B., Karen W., Baby L.,
and all the little cuties
in the world.

1 tiny baby starts to run.

Along comes another...

...to
have
some
fun.

2

silly
babies
spin
around.

Along comes another . . .

3 bouncy babies

...and

she

falls

down.

jump and . . . hop!

Along
comes
another . . .

4 noisy babies

...but he just can't stop!

bang and shout!

Along comes another . . .

...to

sing

right

out!

5 jiggly

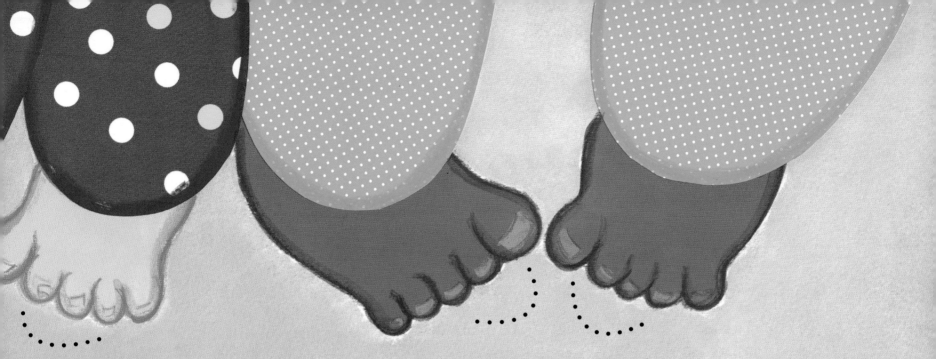

babies wriggle their toes.

Along
comes
another...

6 hungry babies

...who wiggles her nose!

sip and chew.

Along
comes
another...

7 dirty babies

. . . she'll
nibble
some
too!

scrub-a-dub.

Along
comes
another...

8 cuddly babies

. . . straight

into

the tub.

put their pj's on.

Along comes another...

9 drowsy babies

. . .with
a
big,
sleepy
yawn.

crawl to bed.

Along comes another . . .

10 tiny babies without

...to
rest
her
head.

a peep. . .

. . . all **10**

babies are fast asleep!

Good night, babies!